Let's Go!

4 Easy-to-Read Books

Hello, School Bus!
Hello, Fire Truck!
Hello, Freight Train!
Little Red Caboose

SCHOLASTIC INC.

Cartwheel
·B·O·O·K·S·®

New York Toronto London Auckland Sydney
Mexico City New Delhi Hong Kong Buenos Aires

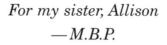

For my sister, Allison
—M.B.P.

To Bobby and Curtis
—B.K.

Hello, School Bus! (0-439-59889-3)
Text copyright © 2004 by Marjorie Blain Parker.
Illustrations copyright © 2004 by Bob Kolar.

Hello, Fire Truck! (0-439-59890-7)
Text copyright © 2004 by Marjorie Blain Parker.
Illustrations copyright © 2004 by Bob Kolar.

Hello, Freight Train! (0-439-59891-5)
Text copyright © 2005 by Marjorie Blain Parker.
Illustrations copyright © 2005 by Bob Kolar.

Little Red Caboose (0-590-63598-0)
Text copyright © 1940, 1967 by Carl Fischer, Inc.
Copyright renewed. All rights reserved. Used by permission.
Illustrations copyright © 1998 by Jill Dubin.
Note: This text is an adaptation of a popular children's song.

ISBN: 0-439-76315-0

12 11 10 9 8 7 6 5 4 3 2   5 6 7 8 9 10/0
Printed in Singapore 46 • This compilation edition first printing, June 2005

Hello, School Bus!

by **Marjorie Blain Parker**
Illustrated by **Bob Kolar**

We wave.
We meet.
We watch and wait.

Yes! Here it comes!
We won't be late.

Hello, school bus!

Lights flash. Cars stop.

Doors open wide.

The driver smiles.
"Come on inside!"

3

The bus is big,

yellow, and black.

We climb the steps.

We walk to the back.

**Doors shut. Brakes hiss.
"Quick! Grab a seat!"**

Ready, set, go!
We roll down the street.

Wheels bump. Kids bounce.

There's lots of noise!

The bus fills up
with girls and boys.

We play. We joke.

We sing and shout.

We are at school.
It's time to get out.

Good-bye, school bus!

Hello, Fire Truck!

Hello, Fire Truck!

by **Marjorie Blain Parker**
Illustrated by **Bob Kolar**

Look—
smoke and flames.
Fluff is in trouble.

Call 911!
Quick—on the double!

Sirens and lights say, "Out of my way!"

Firefighters race
to help save the day.

Hello, fire truck!

51

The truck is red
and shiny and bright.

The team is brave and ready to fight.

Hurry! Hurry!
The fire is growing!

Hoses and pumps
get water flowing.

Rescue ladders climb higher and higher....

Now Fluff is down, safe from the fire.

The fire is out.
The crew packs
the gear.

Tired and dirty,
they wave
as we cheer.

Good-bye, fire truck.

Hello, Freight Train!

For my brother Robert — who's always going somewhere
—M.B.P.

For Elliot, Avery, and Adelan
— B.K.

Hello, Freight Train!

by **Marjorie Blain Parker**
Illustrated by **Bob Kolar**

Lights flash and bells ring.
Down, down goes the gate.

**Here comes the freight train.
We watch as we wait.**

**The engine is first,
so bold and so strong.**

It pulls all the cars that follow along.

Hello, freight train!

Here comes a flat car, a hopper, a rack car.

Here comes a boxcar,
and a big piggyback car . .

**cars with chickens,
cows, and hogs,**

cars with lumber,
coal, and logs.

Tank cars for gas.
Tank cars for oil.

**Refrigerator cars
where food won't spoil.**

The train rolls away,
far down the track.

The last car's light blinks from the back.

Good-bye, freight train!

Little Red Caboose

To Henry, for the smiles
—J.D.

Little Red Caboose

Adapted by **Steve Metzger**
Illustrated by **Jill Dubin**

Little Red Caboose goes
chug chug chug.

Little Red Caboose goes
chug chug chug.

Little Red Caboose is
behind the train.

A smokestack is on its back.

It's chugging down the track.

Little Red Caboose is
behind the train.

Little Red Caboose goes
chug chug chug.

Little Red Caboose goes
chug chug chug.

Little Red Caboose
moves very fast.

It watches trees go by.

It watches birds that fly.

Little Red Caboose
moves very fast.

Little Red Caboose goes
chug chug chug.

Little Red Caboose goes
chug chug chug.

Little Red Caboose
moves through the dark.

It sees the stars at night.
It sees the moon so bright.

Little Red Caboose
moves through the dark.

Little Red Caboose goes
chug chug chug.

Little Red Caboose goes
chug chug chug.

Little Red Caboose is
behind the train.

It's hanging on the end.
It's coming round the bend.

Little Red Caboose is
behind the train.